The Story of the Root-Children

Sibylle von Olfers

Floris Books

Under the ground, deep in the earth among the roots of the trees, the little root-children were fast asleep all winter long. They felt nothing of the biting wind, the cold snow or the stinging hailstorms. They slept peacefully in their warm burrows. They were dreaming of the sunshine in which they had played all through the summer. And what wonderful dreams they were!

When at last winter came to an end and the sun began to melt the snow, Mother Earth came along with her candle to wake them up again.

"Wake up, children," she called kindly. "Time to get up now. You've slept long enough. Spring is coming and there's work to be done. I've brought you scissors, needles and thread and pieces of cloth so that you can all make new clothes. Wake up! As soon as you're ready, I'll unlock and open the doors up to the ground."

The children yawned and stretched. Then they jumped up merrily. Hurray, spring is coming!

Mother Earth had pieces of lovely coloured cloth in her basket. Each of the root-children chose her own colour to make a dress. The snowdrop chose a snow-white cloth, the forget-me-not a sky-blue piece, the buttercup bright yellow, the daisy white with yellow and a bit of red, and the poppy a bright red.

Then they sat down in a cosy circle and began to work busily. They cut, they sewed and pressed until everything fitted exactly. And, as they worked, they sang all the spring songs that they knew.

As soon as they had finished making their new dresses, they went up to Mother Earth in a long procession. Mother Earth looked over her spectacles in surprise when she saw the root-children coming so soon.

"Well, well, you have been quick," she exclaimed, "and how nice it all looks!"

Even the little ants who had been helping Mother Earth to wind up her wool came to look inquisitively. They had never seen such splendid clothes.

But there was still more to be done. The ladybirds, the beetles, the grubs and the bumble-bees had also been sleeping under the ground and had now woken up. They had to be washed and brushed, painted colourfully and made to shine so that they would look as beautiful as possible. What a hustle and bustle was going on down there!

Up above ground, the warm sun was already bringing out the new green leaves on the trees. Would the root-children be ready in time?

At last it was really springtime! Mother Earth opened the door. Then out into the lovely warm spring sunshine came the stately procession of beetles, lady-birds and root-children with their blades of grass and flowers.

In the wood, the butterflies fluttered happily around the flowers. The lilies-of-the-valley found a cool spot in the shade of the trees beside the blue violet and there they let their flower-bells tinkle.

There too old father Sliffslaff-Slibberslak came slowly creeping along.

"Ha, there you all are! Welcome to the big forest," he called to the children.

The little violet looked at him shyly from her safe place behind her tree. She had never seen such a creature before!

Summer came. In the little brook that flowed between the meadows, the water-lily let herself be carried over the water like a princess.

The reeds whispered in the wind. The forget-me-nots came and stepped carefully into the water. But the beetles grumbled:

"It's getting too crowded here. Go and play somewhere else!"

In the flower-meadows, the root-children were having a high time. They danced nimbly in the warm sunshine. Hop and skip, whoopee, what fun! If only it were always summer!

The butterflies fluttered above them, and even the beetle risked a dance. The crickets chirped, the bees buzzed and that was their music.

"Mind out, little grass, don't fall down!"

But summer also came to an end. The sharp autumn wind whirled the brightly coloured leaves through the air and tugged at the root-children's clothes.

"Hoo," called the wind, "hurry home, it's getting cold here. It's time to go to bed."

So then they all went back again in a long procession. Mother Earth was standing by the door and hugged each child one by one.

"Come in, children," she said, "and you too, beetles and bees. It's warm and cosy in here and I've got something for you all to eat and drink. After that you must all go to sleep until I wake you up again in the springtime."

And all the little root-children went down under the ground again to start their long winter's sleep.

Sibylle von Olfers

Sibylle von Olfers' (1881–1916) blend of natural observation and use of simple design has led to comparisons with Kate Greenaway and Elsa Beskow.

She was born the third of five children in a castle in East Prussia. Encouraged by her aunt, she trained at art college. Her beauty attracted many admirers and suitors, but she remained aloof and distant from the "useless world of the aristocrats."

At the age of twenty-five she joined the Sisters of Saint Elisabeth, an order of nuns. As well as teaching art in the local school, she wrote and illustrated a number of children's books. Tragically she died at the age of thirty-four from a lung infection.

Her first book is *The Story of the Snow Children,* published in 1905, followed by *The Story of the Root Children* (1906), *Princess in the Forest* (1909) and *The Story of the Wind Children* (1910).